TERRY DEARY

PIRATE TALES
THE PIRATE CAPTAIN

Illustrated by Helen Flook

BLOOMSBURY EDUCATION
AN IMPRINT OF BLOOMSBURY

LONDON OXFORD NEW YORK NEW DELHI SYDNEY

CHAPTER ONE
SEAS AND SLAUGHTER

The North Atlantic, 1726

Captain Fly was a small man. Not as small as a fly, of course, but not much larger than a boy.

"I am the terror of the Atlantic Ocean!" he boasted. "In fact, I may be the greatest terror of the seven seas!"

"What seas are those, then, Captain?" his greasy-haired, bare-footed, bear-brained, bullying mate Mr Blood wanted to know.

"Seas?"

"Yes, Captain Fly. What are the *seven* seas?" Blood asked.

"Well, there's the North Atlantic... and the *South* Atlantic, of course."

"Of course," his ugly friend Mr Slaughter nodded. "But what about the other five?"

"The Pacific Ocean... and that makes *seven*."

"Three," Mr Blood corrected.

Fly turned as red as a cockerel's comb. He waved his short, dirty fingers under Blood's nose and counted. "North... one... Atlantic... two... South... three... Atlantic... four... The... five... Pacific... six... Ocean... seven. Seven seas, *see*?"

"Suppose," Mr Blood grumbled.

"Suppose?" Captain Fly sneered. "Nobody argues with William Fly. I was a boxing champion, you know."

"I know."

"And I'll batter anybody that argues with me." The captain turned suddenly towards Slaughter. "You're bigger than me, Slaughter, but I could batter you."

He waved a fist under the sailor's broken nose. "I'm fast. Fast Fly they used to call me in the boxing ring. Champion of America, I was. Fast Fly."

"Too fast for me, Captain," Slaughter chuckled. "Too fast for any man on the three seas."

"Seven seas," Fly said.

"Yes, them as well."

Captain Fly turned back to Blood. "Now fetch the prisoners on deck. It's time I gave them their orders."

CHAPTER TWO
BLOOD AND BATTER

Mr Blood opened a hatch in the deck of the rolling ship. Five men and a boy blinked in the sunlight.

"Up on deck, you scurvy lot. Captain Fly wants to give you your orders."

The men had been crowded into a small space for over an hour and they were stiff.

"Hurry it up," Seaman Slaughter shouted. "Nobody keeps Captain Fly waiting... or, if they do, he batters them. Batter, batter, batter," Slaughter said, and made punching movements with his fat fists.

Most of the prisoners looked afraid. But one man stood taller than the rest and he just looked amused. He held a trembling skinny boy by the hand and muttered,

"It'll be all right, young Arthur. I'll not let them hurt you."

Slaughter pushed them into a line. "Right, prisoners. Silence while Captain Fly speaks."

Fly climbed up onto the aft deck so he could look down his twisted nose at the miserable men. He gave a black-toothed grin. "You're a lucky bunch, you are. When we captured your ship this morning, we took your tobacco load and then we sank the old tub. Any other pirate would have sunk you with it. But not me. Not Captain Fly. I'm too kind for that."

The tall prisoner stepped forward. "A kind man wouldn't have robbed us in the first place," he said.

Fly turned purple with anger. "Nobody argues with William Fly. I was a boxing champion, you know, and I'll batter anyone that argues with me. What's your name?"

"Captain Jed Atkinson," the tall man said. "I'm captain of the ship you villains just sank."

Fly threw back his head and laughed a mad laugh. "Ha! Ha! Hahhhhh! You are not *captain* any longer. There's room for only *one* captain on a ship, and the captain of *Fame's Revenge* is me. And if anyone ever calls *you* captain on board *my* ship, I'll feed him to the sharks. Understand?"

"There are not many sharks on the east coast of America," Jed Atkinson said quietly.

Captain Fly pretended he hadn't heard. "As I was saying, I am the kindest pirate you'll ever have the good luck to meet. My ship is short of crew, and you are sailors, so I kept you alive to help me."

"What happened to the rest of your crew?" the boy said in a trembling voice. "Did you feed them to the sharks?"

Fly glared at him. "No. No... they got so rich with their share of the treasure, they retired. And that's what *you* will do, too. Serve me for a year, and I'll make you as rich as a king. But try to escape, and I'll batter you."

"He'll batter you. Batter, batter, batter," Seaman Slaughter said, and laughed. "Hur, hur, hur!"

CHAPTER THREE
SLAVES AND SHARKS

"We're slaves," young Arthur groaned. His red-brown hair had been cut with a blunt knife and it was as shaggy as a bear.

"Slaves?" Jed smiled. "For a while..."

"Forever," the boy said.

Jed hauled on the ropes to raise the sail and head north. The coast of North Carolina was a grey-green smudge on the horizon. "We have a lot going for us, Arthur."

"What? He's a champion boxer... we can't fight him. Even if we did, he has Blood and Slaughter to help him. And they have pistols."

tall man tied the rope and turned to the boy. "No sailor can stay at sea for ever. He has to go into port at least once a month. There'll be lots of chances to escape."

"But Blood and Slaughter..."

"...are as stupid as William Fly. We'll have lots of chances to trick them."

Arthur's face brightened and he wiped away the tears. "When, Captain Atkinson?"

"Don't call me captain, remember? Call me Jed."

"Yes, Captain," the boy promised. "What's your plan?"

"The first part of the plan is to work hard. Get Fly to trust us. Do exactly what he says. Look as if we're happy," Jed said.

"And rob other ships? But the navy might catch us and hang us along with the real pirates," Arthur sighed.

"We don't have a lot of choice. If we refuse to help, he'll throw us overboard... to feed the sharks that aren't there."

"And the second part of your plan?"

"Wait and see. I'll tell you when the time comes."

"What are you two muttering about?" Seaman Slaughter asked as he marched down the deck.

Arthur stepped forward to meet him. "We were just saying how lucky we are to have been captured by you and Captain Fly. We can't wait to start boarding ships and getting rich."

"Can't you?" the ugly sailor grunted.

"Captain Fly is the greatest pirate to sail the Atlantic," Jed Atkinson put in.

"The greatest to sail the seven seas," Slaughter told him.

"What seas are those?" Arthur asked.

"Erm... North Atlantic, South Atlantic and the Pacific Ocean," Slaughter told him.

"That's only three," Arthur said.

Slaughter shook his head. "Captain Fly says it's seven, so it must be seven," he said, and walked away.

Arthur looked at Jed Atkinson. "You're right, Captain – about as stupid as they come."

CHAPTER FOUR
SAILS AND SANDBANKS

The first ship that young Arthur robbed was a cutter not much larger than the rowing boat of *Fame's Revenge*. It was sailing close to the shore with sacks of grain and packets of food on deck.

The skipper saw *Fame's Revenge* heading towards him and tried to raise more sail. "Blow him out of the water!" Captain Fly screeched.

His crew ran towards the three cannon he had on the deck and pulled them to the side of the schooner.

Jed Atkinson spoke quietly. "If you sink him, you won't get his cargo, Captain Fly."

"I know that," the pirate replied. He turned to the men hauling the cannon.

"Don't be so stupid – if we sink him, we won't get his cargo – put on more sail. Raise the main gaff topsail," he ordered.

The men let go of the cannon, which started to roll across the slippery deck and crunch into the side. The sailors scrambled over an untidy tangle of ropes and sails and got in one another's way.

Arthur looked at Jed. "He's not a very good sailor, is he?"

"Hopeless," the tall man agreed.

The cutter was starting to sail away. Captain Fly was jumping up and down on the spot. "Get that mainsail up. He's escaping."

"I thought you said the main gaff topsail," Slaughter reminded him.

"Never mind what I said... just do it."

"Urrrr?" Blood grunted.

Suddenly, Jed Atkinson stepped towards the main mast and picked up a rope. He turned to the men who had sailed with him on his own ship. "Muller and Finch, Adams and Bishop... get these ropes sorted. Untie the sails in the right order."

"Yes, Captain Atkinson," Jan Muller said with a grin and the sailors worked quickly like the team they used to be.

"Take this rope, Slaughter," Jed said calmly. "You, Blood, haul this mainsail first... that's right... now, Slaughter, the main gaff topsail's free... it'll go up next."

Slaughter smiled a green-toothed smile. "So it does, Captain."

"He's not a captain!" Fly raged. "I told you not to call him captain or you'll be thrown over the side."

"I'll throw myself over the side when we're on the beach," Slaughter promised. "Look, Captain Fly, we're getting closer to the cutter now."

"And we're getting closer to the sandbanks," Jed said. "Take the rudder, Arthur," he ordered the red-haired boy. "Steer to starboard... that's the way. I know these waters, and we'll run aground in a ship this big. The captain of the cutter knows that. He's trying to lead us into a trap."

"A trap, a trap!" Fly shrieked. "I knew it. Just as well you have me to save your scurvy lives!" he cried.

"We're in a deep channel now," Jed Atkinson said a few minutes later. "Hard to port, Arthur, and we'll cut him off. He'll have to stop."

"Cut off the cutter... cutter him off," Fly screamed, and ran to the bow of his schooner to watch as they neared the trading ship. The victim began to run down his sails and slow down, defeated.

"Now lower the sails," Jed shouted to his crew. "That's the way... gaff topsail first... mainsail next. Gently to starboard, Arthur."

Fame's Revenge drifted alongside the cutter and the glum trader threw a line to Slaughter, who hauled the two ships side by side.

"I did it," Fly crowed. "I did it!"

Chapter Five
Pancakes and Poverty

"What do you have on board?" Captain Fly called to the skipper of the cutter.

The miserable man and his three gloomy crew looked up. "Supplies for my shop in Wilmington... not much. I can't afford much. Just a couple of sacks of cornflour, salt, butter, a barrel of wine and one of molasses."

"What's molasses?" Captain Fly asked.

"It's what you call treacle back in England," Slaughter explained.

"Not much of a treasure," Arthur muttered, a little too loudly.

"We'll eat well for a week," Fly said angrily.

Blood scratched his head through greasy hair and pulled out a louse. "Cornflour and treacle? We can't eat cornflour and treacle."

"No... no..." Captain Fly huffed. "We bake the cornflour into bread."

"There isn't an oven on this schooner, Captain Fly," Slaughter reminded him.

Just as Fly was about to explode, Jed stepped forward. "Young Arthur was the galley boy on our ship. He can turn cornflour into wonderful pancakes over the hotplate."

"Ha! See?" Fly smirked. "We can have pancakes... lovely with treacle, they are. My mum used to fry them back in Bristol. Lovely. Now, load them onto *Fame's Revenge*," he ordered.

That evening, the schooner sat at anchor and the crew ate a mountain of pancakes that Arthur made. They sat around the main mast and washed the meal down with wine.

Jed turned to Captain Fly. "So how did you get into pirating, Captain?" he asked.

Fly breathed in deeply so his skinny chest blew out like a bullfrog's. "I gave up boxing in Bristol to join a slave-trader, Captain Green. We bought slaves in Africa and sold them in Jamaica for ten times the price."

"A good deal," Jed said and gave a glance of disgust towards Arthur.

"It would have been better if so many slaves hadn't died on the trip," Fly spat.

"But Captain Green was a cruel man. He had his crew flogged at the drop of a hat."

"Is that where you learned to be cruel?" Arthur asked.

Fly's eyes glowed as he remembered. "One night, my friends, Blood and Slaughter, dropped old Green on an island in the Atlantic and I took over *Fame's Revenge*. I gave up the slaving – all those Atlantic storms were ruining my ship. I decided to pirate off the coast of Carolina – there are so many little ships that run up and down from Dismal Swamp down to Cape Fear. It's an easy life."

"Bullying little ships and driving them into poverty," Jed said quietly.

"That was two weeks ago, Atkinson, and you were my first prize. Easy," Fly crowed.

"Easy when you have a couple of cannon," Jed agreed.

"Easy," Fly nodded and his head fell forward onto his chest. He snored.

When the wine sent Blood and Slaughter to sleep, too, Jed Atkinson wandered over to check the anchor chain at the front. When he was sure Fly's crew were not going to wake up, he gave a small signal for his own men to join him. Muller and Finch, Adams and Bishop crept forward with young Arthur.

"Yes?" Dick Adams asked quietly. "Do you have a plan to get us off this Hell-ship?"

"I have a plan," their true captain replied.

Arthur felt a glow of happiness warm him deep inside.

CHAPTER SIX
FLAG AND FLIGHT

The next morning was cool and windy. *Fame's Revenge* rocked and creaked as it wallowed in the water, waiting. Captain Fly was too lazy to sail out to seek his victims.

"We sit here and let them come to us," he told his crew. "That's what a great pirate would do. Pass me a pancake, young Arthur."

He was eating his third pancake of the morning and grease was dribbling into his scrawny beard when Muller called down from the top of the mast, "Brig trading ship to the east, Captain Fly."

Fly looked around at the crew. "Well? What are you waiting for?"

"For orders, Captain Fly," Dick Adams told him.

Fly shook his ugly head. "Run a flag to the top of the mast. A flag of distress to show we're in trouble," he said slowly, as if he were talking to a child.

"But we aren't in trouble, Captain," Slaughter said.

Fly rolled his eyes. "No, but the brig will come to our rescue. As soon as she comes alongside, we'll capture her, understand?"

"No," Slaughter said.

"It's... a... *trick*, Slaughter. Saves us the trouble of chasing the brig."

"Oh, I see," Blood grinned. "Clever Captain Fly. A trick!"

"Oh, I get it," Slaughter said with a gap-toothed smile. "Hur! Hur! Hur!"

Seaman Bishop found a white flag with a red cross. He tied it to a rope and pulled until the flag slid up the mast.

The crew watched as the brig drew closer. As soon as it was half a mile away, it raised its sails and turned away.

"What's happening?" Fly cried.

"He's running away from us, Captain," Blood replied.

"But we need help!" Fly wailed.

"No, we don't," Slaughter argued.

"He *thinks* we do," the captain raged.

Jed Atkinson sighed. "That's Martin Paris's ship – he's not a fool. He knows it's a trick."

Fly jumped to his feet. "After him, Atkinson. After him. Catch him. Blow him out of the water. Hurry!"

Jed Atkinson took command. He gave the orders and turned *Fame's Revenge* to race after the brig.

"I'll kill them," Fly shouted. "I'll batter them all when I catch them."

Fame's Revenge reared up like a wild horse and set off on the chase.

CHAPTER SEVEN
FAME AND FORTUNE

Jed Atkinson made sure *Fame's Revenge* soon caught Martin Paris's brig.

Captain Fly ran across the deck and stood behind a loaded cannon. "Surrender... surrender or die!" he called and waved a lighted fuse over the cannon.

Captain Martin Paris spread his hands. "What do you want?" he asked.

"All your gold and all your silver. Your pistols... and your pancakes," the little Englishman cried.

Paris shook his head sadly. "If you bring your ship too close, we'll break up... the sea's too rough today. You'll have to send over a rowing boat to pick up our money," he called back. The captain wore his grey hair pulled back into a pigtail that was made stiff with tar.

"Lower the boat, Adams and Bishop," Fly ordered. "Row across and rob their riches."

Adams and Bishop moved slowly towards the rowing boat that was stowed on the deck. They fastened a rope on each end and, with the help of Muller and Finch, they lowered it into the frothing water.

Young Arthur stepped forward quickly. He was trembling. He had to get his part in the plot right. "No, Captain Fly... you can't let Adams and Bishop go. They'll jump onto Captain Paris's ship and escape. You can't trust them."

"Oh, no," Adams groaned, very loud. *Too* loud, Arthur thought. He was acting his part a bit too hard. "Oh, no... that cursed boy has ruined our plan. Our plan to escape."

"Oh, no," Seaman Bishop sighed, even louder.

"Aha!" Captain Fly laughed. "You can't trick a cunning pirate like William Fly, my lads. I saw through your plan. I'm not going to let you row off to freedom."

Adams and Bishop hung their heads and tried to look sad.

"What do we do then?" Slaughter asked.

"Well, it's as clear as the nose on your face, Slaughter," Fly laughed.

There was silence for a moment. Just the slapping of waves against the side of *Fame's Revenge*.

"Well?" Blood asked. "What *do* we do?"

"Ha! Ha! Hahhhhh!" Fly laughed. "What do we do? You're an idiot, Blood." He looked over his shoulder. "Tell him what we do, Jed Atkinson."

Jed gave a soft smile. "Even young Arthur knows what we do. Tell Seaman Blood, lad."

Arthur nodded. "We send Captain Fly's most trusted men across to the brig. Give Slaughter and Blood all the pistols we have and let them row across," the boy told Fly.

"See? Idiot. You and Slaughter row across... here, take my pistol. Don't come back without my fortune."

"*Your* fortune, Captain Fly?" Slaughter said with a frown.

"*Our* fortune, I meant to say. Now hurry. I can't wait to run my fingers through a chest full of gold."

CHAPTER EIGHT
ROPE AND REVENGE

Slaughter and Blood climbed down the rope at the side of *Fame's Revenge* and fell into the rowing boat with a clunk. They were clumsy sailors and it took them a while to untangle themselves from the oars and set off towards Martin Paris's ship.

Jed Atkinson walked over to the side of *Fame's Revenge* and waved at Captain Paris. "Hello there, Martin, are you well?"

Paris scowled. "Jed Atkinson turned pirate? I can't believe it!"

"No, Martin, I was a prisoner of Captain Fly. Now I want you to do me a small favour, old friend."

"What's that?"

"Sail in to the harbour at Wilmington and tell them we're bringing in the pirate Captain Fly – they can arrest him as soon as we land. We don't want them firing at *Fame's Revenge* when we enter the harbour."

Martin Paris saluted and gave orders for his crew to set sail for Wilmington.

William Fly listened with his mouth open. "Arrest? Arrest me? You can't do that – I'll batter you." He raised his fists and jumped forward. He stepped into a loop of rope that Arthur had laid on the deck.

As Fly's foot went into the noose, Arthur pulled it tight. Fly tripped and fell on his face, roaring with anger. Muller and Finch, Adams and Bishop grabbed an end of the rope, threw it over a spar and hauled on it so Captain Fly was hanging by his foot.

"Blood and Slaughter..." he choked. "Where are Blood and Slaughter, my trusty friends?"

Arthur looked at the upside-down captain who thrashed like a cod on a fishing line. "They're in the Atlantic Ocean in a rowing boat. Captain Paris sailed off before they reached him, and we're sailing off before they can get back here."

"You killed my pirates... they can't row all the way back to Carolina... we're ten miles off the coast!" Fly cried.

"It's all right," Jed Atkinson said with a smile. "We'll hand you over and then we'll send the navy out in a frigate to pick them up. You can all share a cosy jail cell until your trial."

"Ooooh! I don't want to share a cell with those two – they smell like rotting fish. Ooooh! What have I done to deserve this?" the little man wailed.

"Been a pirate," Arthur said. "And that's what happens to all pirates in the end."

CHAPTER NINE
CUTTER AND BUTTER

Jed Atkinson called to Muller and Finch, Adams and Bishop, "Raise the mainsail. Arthur... steady north-west. We'll catch that cutter in half an hour."

Atkinson walked across the deck of *Fame's Revenge* proudly. Captain Fly had sunk his old ship. But the judge had given Jed *Fame's Revenge* as a reward for capturing William Fly.

The little cutter battled through the waves, but it was no match for the big pirate ship and its expert crew. At last the small boat lowered its mast and the captain turned to face his enemy.

"You robbed us last month, William Fly," the man sighed. "We've nothing left worth stealing. Just a few sacks of corn. My family will starve if you rob us again."

Arthur lashed the steering oar tight and joined his captain at the starboard side of the ship. "I'm Captain Jed Atkinson. William Fly's in prison," he shouted across the lapping water.

The captain of the cutter shrugged. "You're still a pirate, whatever you call yourself. And I'm just a shopkeeper that you've ruined. My wife says we'll be eating the leather from our boots if I don't bring these sacks of corn back home safe."

Jed Atkinson grinned. "Fly took two sacks of cornflour from you, salt, butter, a barrel of wine and one of molasses. We're here to give them back." He turned to his crew and ordered them to start unloading supplies from *Fame's Revenge* onto the little cutter.

The shopkeeper watched and his mouth fell open. "My wife will be... she'll be – " he began. But tears choked his throat and he just sniffled as he watched the hold of his ship fill up. Arthur helped load the last of the barrels and sacks before climbing back into *Fame's Revenge*.

Jed waved goodbye, ran back to the steering oar and finally the shopkeeper found his voice. He called across, "A pirate captain that *gives* to his victims? You're like King Arthur and... and his knights of the Round Table. Knights of the sea. What's your name, young sir?"

Arthur threw back his head and laughed the way William Fly had once laughed. "Ha! Ha! Hahhhhh! King Arthur, of course."

And the *Fame's Revenge* headed west into the setting sun to find more good deeds to do.

EPILOGUE

William Fly was a cruel captain who robbed traders off the American coast in his ship *Fame's Revenge*. The men who sailed his ships were mostly victims he had captured. In the end he was tricked by these men, who wanted their own revenge.

William Fly was born in England. His life as a pirate started when he led a rebellion on the slave ship Elizabeth. The ship had been sailing to West Africa. Fly and his friends threw the captain into the sea to drown.

After they'd captured the ship, Fly and his rebels made a Jolly Roger flag, and changed the name of the ship to *Fame's Revenge.*

The rebels decided to make William Fly their captain. They sold the slaves and then sailed to the coast of North Carolina. They captured five ships in a couple of months and the Carolina traders were terrified.

Fly had a terrible temper and if his enemies upset him he would have them whipped a hundred times. His pirate life didn't make him rich – although he robbed ships of tobacco, cloth, logs or spices.

Captain Fly captured Captain Atkinson from a trading ship and forced him to slave as a member of his crew. Atkinson was a good crew member but he was really waiting for his chance to rebel. It came when they attacked a schooner and Fly's most trusted men went off to board it.

Atkinson and his captured comrades turned the tables on Fly and took him prisoner. They sailed him off to prison. Fly had been a pirate for only two months.

You try

1. Shanty time

Pirates were like most sailors and liked to sing as they worked. Their songs are known as 'shanties'. They tell a story and have lines that everyone could join in.

When a popular captain called Captain Storm died, a shanty was written about him:

He was a sailor bold and true,
Aye, aye, aye, storm a-long!
A good old skipper to his crew;
Aye, aye, aye, Mister Storm a-long.

Of captains brave he was the best,
Aye, aye, aye, storm a-long!
But now he's gone and is at rest;
Aye, aye, aye, Mister Storm a-long.

Can you write some more verses for this shanty? In each verse, remember:

- the first line rhymes with the third line
- line 2 is always *Aye, aye, aye, storm a-long!*
- the last line of each verse is always *Aye, aye, aye, Mister Storm a-long.*

2. Pirate rules

Pirates were lawless men, but they had their own rules. Some rules made sure they were always ready to fight:

> You must keep your pistols and cutlass
> clean and fit for service.

Some tried to make sure they didn't argue among themselves and get into fights:

> You must not play cards or dice for money.

And the strangest one made sure they were fit to do battle by getting plenty of sleep:

> Your lights and candles are to be
> put out at eight o'clock at night.

Imagine YOU are a pirate captain! Make a poster for all your crew to see, giving ten rules you think they should obey.